The Mystery of Case D. Luc

Beverly Lewis

Beverly Lewis Books for Young Readers

PICTURE BOOKS

In Jesse's Shoes • *Just Like Mama*
What Is God Like? • *What Is Heaven Like?*

THE CUL-DE-SAC KIDS

The Double Dabble Surprise
The Chicken Pox Panic
The Crazy Christmas Angel Mystery
No Grown-ups Allowed
Frog Power
The Mystery of Case D. Luc
The Stinky Sneakers Mystery
Pickle Pizza
Mailbox Mania
The Mudhole Mystery
Fiddlesticks
The Crabby Cat Caper
Tarantula Toes
Green Gravy
Backyard Bandit Mystery
Tree House Trouble
The Creepy Sleep-Over
The Great TV Turn-Off
Piggy Party
The Granny Game
Mystery Mutt
Big Bad Beans
The Upside-Down Day
The Midnight Mystery

Katie and Jake and the Haircut Mistake

www.BeverlyLewis.com

THE CUL-DE-SAC KIDS

The Mystery of Case D. Luc

Beverly Lewis

BETHANY HOUSE PUBLISHERS
MINNEAPOLIS, MINNESOTA 55438

© 1995 by Beverly Lewis

Published by Bethany House Publishers
11400 Hampshire Avenue South
Bloomington, Minnesota 55438
www.bethanyhouse.com

Bethany House Publishers is a division of
Baker Publishing Group, Grand Rapids, MI

Printed in the United States of America by
Bethany Press International, Bloomington, MN
November 2012, 22nd printing

ISBN 978–1–55661–646–4

          Library of Congress Cataloging-in-Publication Data
Lewis, Beverly
     The Mystery of Case D. Luc / by Beverly Lewis
          p.   cm.—(The cul-de-sac kids ; 6)
     Summary: Dunkum follows a trail of sercret coded messages to
find his missing autographed basketball.
     ISBN 1–55661–646–5
     [1. Mystery and detective stories.] I. Title. II. Series: Lewis,
Beverly. Cul-de-sac kids ; 6..
PZ7.L58464Myn   1995
[Fic]—dc20   97-22384

Cover illustration by Paul Turnbaugh
Story illustrations by Barbara Birch

12   13   14   15   16   17   18   28   27   26   25   24   23   22

To Carole Billingsley,
who solves word puzzles
faster than warp speed.
Well, almost.

THE CUL-DE-SAC KIDS

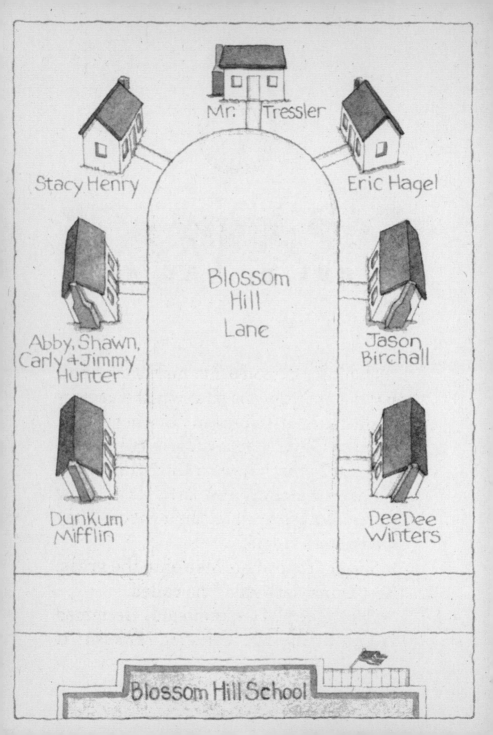

ONE

Dunkum dribbled his new basketball up the driveway. The basketball was very special. David Robinson, his hero, had signed it! David Robinson wasn't just any basketball star, he was a Christian, too.

Jason Birchall and Eric Hagel flew into Dunkum's yard on their bikes. They skidded to a stop.

Jason dropped his bike onto the grass. "Hey, Dunk, let's ride," he called.

"Not today," Dunkum said. He aimed his ball at the net and shot. *Whoosh!* It slipped right through.

"Aw, come on," Eric begged. But Dunkum ignored them and kept shooting baskets.

Soon, Abby Hunter and her little sister Carly showed up. "Hi, Dunkum," Abby said. "Do you have time to talk about the April Fool's Day party?"

Dunkum dribbled the ball under his leg. "Not now." He shot the ball up over his shoulder. It bounced off the backboard. In!

"Good shot, now let's go," Jason said.

Stacy Henry, Abby's best friend, came down the sidewalk. "What's up?" she asked.

"Hi, Stacy," Abby said. "I'm trying to talk to Dunkum about the party next week."

Dunkum stopped shooting baskets. "Sorry, Abby. I have to keep practicing."

"But you practice *all* the time," Eric said.

10

Carly giggled. "If you don't watch out, you'll turn into a basketball!"

"Eric's right," Stacy said. "All you ever do is shoot baskets. What about *us*?"

Dunkum ran between Abby and Carly and shot the ball. It spun off the rim and he chased after it.

"Stop bouncing that silly basketball," Carly said.

Dunkum froze like a statue. "What did you say?"

Jason and Eric began hooting like owls. Eric laughed so hard, his bike toppled over.

Dunkum glared at Carly. "Nobody calls my basketball *silly*! David Robinson wrote his name right here!" He held the ball up for them to see.

Abby shot him a sour look. "Your basketball isn't silly. *You* are!"

"Oh, yeah?" Dunkum felt the back of his neck getting warm.

Stacy walked up to him. "We can't plan

11

our April Fool's Day party because of you. You're too busy with this!" She tapped on his basketball.

Dunkum swung the ball away from her. "Then plan it without me," he said. "I don't care."

"But we always have our meetings at *your* house," Abby said. She was the president of the Cul-de-sac Kids—nine kids on Blossom Hill Lane.

Dunkum dodged Abby, then leaped up and shot. Missed! "Go have your *silly* meeting somewhere else," he said.

Abby frowned. "Please, Dunkum. Just talk to us!"

"Not today," Dunkum said. "I'm busy."

Jason whistled. "That's what he always says!"

"Do not," Dunkum muttered.

"Uh-huh!" Eric shouted. "Maybe you want to drop out of the Cul-de-sac Kids. Is that it?"

Abby frowned. "No, we stick together

13

around here, remember?"

Dunkum didn't care about sticking together. His basketball was more important. He spun the ball on his pointer finger. "I'm going inside," he said, then ran into the house.

Dunkum never even looked back at the Cul-de-sac Kids. Not even once.

TWO

In his room, Dunkum placed the ball on his dresser—in front of the mirror. He sat on his bed and stared. *Maybe this ball will make me a great player,* he thought. *Maybe I'll be as famous as David Robinson!*

Suddenly, he dashed to the window and pushed the curtains back. Abby and Carly were gone. So were Jason and Eric. Dunkum almost wished his friends were still waiting in the driveway.

But then he remembered the girls.

15

They had made fun of his fantastic basketball. *Rats!* thought Dunkum. *Who needs them.*

Later, at bedtime, Dunkum read his Sunday school lesson. The verses were in Matthew 6. "Do not store up for yourselves treasures on earth . . . where thieves break in and steal. But store up for yourselves treasures in heaven. . . ."

Dunkum went to his dresser and reached for his basketball. "Maybe it's okay to store up just *one* treasure on earth," he whispered.

Then he carried the ball to bed and pushed it down between the sheets. Dunkum crawled into bed beside it.

In the darkness, he thought about Abby and Carly Hunter. And Stacy Henry. How dare they call his basketball *silly*?

Reaching over, Dunkum felt the hard, round surface next to him. No thief was going to steal *his* treasure! Soon he fell

16

asleep with his arm around the giant lump.

★ ★ ★

Dunkum kicked the covers off. It was Sunday morning. His basketball was still in bed with him. The Cul-de-sac Kids would die laughing, but he didn't care.

He showered and dressed for church. Then he hurried to the kitchen. "Mm-m, eggs smell good," he told his mother.

His dad passed the salt for the scrambled eggs. Then he held up the crossword puzzle in the paper. "Can you solve this?" his dad asked.

"Looks tough," Dunkum said, studying it.

"Not for your dad," his mother said.

Dunkum nodded. It was true, his dad could solve anything. Especially word puzzles.

Before Dunkum ate a single bite, he prayed. He wished his parents would pray

17

with him. He wished they would go to church, too. Sometimes it was lonely being a Christian.

Not long ago, Abby Hunter and her family were the only ones on Blossom Hill Lane who attended church. Now all the Cul-de-sac Kids were going. God's love was catching. And Abby's van was getting crowded with kids—including Dunkum.

After brushing his teeth, Dunkum dashed upstairs to get his Sunday school lesson and Bible. The memory verse was easy. *Let's see,* thought Dunkum. *There was a treasure on earth and a thief stole it. And there was a heavenly treasure and no thief could snatch it!*

Before he left for church, Dunkum hid his basketball in the closet. He closed the door. Now his treasure would be safe. As safe as the heavenly treasure in the Bible.

THREE

Dunkum hurried to Abby's house. The Cul-de-sac Kids piled into the van. All but Dee Dee Winters.

"Where's Dee Dee?" Dunkum asked.

"Her cat is sick," Carly replied.

"That's strange. I saw her cat outside yesterday," Dunkum said.

"Maybe Mister Whiskers ate one of Dee Dee's cookies," Jason teased.

Carly stuck up for her friend. "Dee Dee's cookies are the best in the world!"

"Seat belts, everyone," Abby's father

said before starting the van.

★ ★ ★

After church, Abby's van pulled back into their driveway. She grabbed Dunkum's arm as they climbed out of the van. "We're having a club meeting. Right now! Before you start practicing your shots again."

"Make it quick," Dunkum said. His thoughts were on his new basketball.

Abby called the rest of the kids. They gathered in a circle on her porch. "Next Friday is April Fool's Day. I'm having a party after school," she said. "For all the Cul-de-sac Kids."

"Where?" Stacy asked.

"Let's have it outside," Eric suggested.

"At the end of the cul-de-sac," Carly said.

"Yes!" said Shawn, Abby's adopted Korean brother. "Beside big oak tree."

20

Jason Birchall danced a jig. "What's to eat?"

Abby's eyes twinkled. She pulled a list out of her Sunday purse. "Here's the menu. Remember, it's an April Fool's Day party." She began to read. "First we'll have ants on a log."

"Ants?" squealed Carly. "I'm not eating ants!"

"Next is silly dillies," said Abby, laughing.

"I know what *that* is," Jason said.

"Don't tell." Abby continued, "Number three is garden Popsicles."

"Mm-m," said Eric. "Sounds good."

Stacy held her hands over her ears. "Don't tell me, I want to be surprised."

"Next," said Abby. "We'll have jitter blocks."

Carly giggled. "Must be something wiggly."

"Last of all, we'll have sweet hearts," Abby said.

21

Dunkum frowned. "I thought it was an April Fool's Day party, not a Valentine party."

"Who cares," said Jason. "Sweets are good any day."

"You better stay away from them," said Dunkum. "Remember Valentine's Day, when you pigged out on chocolates?"

Jason groaned and held his stomach. He remembered.

"Hey, Abby, what are jitter blocks?" Dunkum asked.

Abby smiled. "April Fool's Day food, that's what."

Jason and Eric poked each other, laughing.

Jimmy Hunter, Abby's little Korean brother, tugged on the list. "I not like that American food."

Abby hugged him. "It's just for fun," she said. "You'll see."

Stacy grinned. "What will we do at the party besides eat strange food?"

Dunkum had an idea. "We could play basketball."

The kids groaned.

"Not *that* again!" Carly shouted.

"Then I'm not coming," Dunkum said. And he leaped off the porch and headed home.

FOUR

Dunkum's friends called to him, but he kept running. He was sick of planning parties. He was dying to practice basketball.

As he turned toward his house, he heard Dee Dee Winters calling. She lived across the street.

Dunkum spun around. "What do you want?" he grumbled.

"Come over here," she called from her front door.

Dunkum stomped across the street.

Dee Dee was holding her sick cat. "Did you get me a Sunday school paper?"

"I'm not in your class," Dunkum replied.

"Well, *I* got one for you when *you* were sick. That's what friends are supposed to do." Then she asked, "What was your memory verse today?"

"It was two verses, Matthew 6:19 and 20," Dunkum said. "Read it for yourself."

"I already did," Dee Dee answered.

Dunkum shook his head. "Then why did you ask me?"

She grinned. "Just checking."

Dee Dee's as sick as her cat, thought Dunkum. He stormed down the steps and dashed across the street. *Ka-bang!* Dunkum slammed his front door.

Upstairs, he ran to his room and threw open the closet door. He reached for his basketball. It was gone!

Dunkum searched the back of the

26

closet. He looked behind his overnight bag.

"Mom! Dad!" Dunkum called. He ran downstairs, darting in and out of the kitchen. He checked the family room. The house was empty.

Then he remembered. The front door was *unlocked* when he came in. "That's it! A thief walked right into my house and stole my basketball!"

Dunkum didn't bother to check if anything else was missing. He could think of only one thing—his basketball.

Running back upstairs, Dunkum searched everywhere. He looked under his bed. Nothing.

He looked in the hamper. Nope.

He even looked behind the shower curtain. But his ball was nowhere to be found.

Dunkum fell on his bed. The lump in his throat grew and grew. He could hardly swallow. When he did, tears filled his eyes. But he squeezed his eyes shut and wiped the tears away.

He got up and marched downstairs, wondering where his parents were. Looking on the counter, Dunkum spotted a note.

Dear Dunkum,
    We'll be back in a jiffy. We went to get fried chicken. I hope you're hungry!

                    Love ya,
                    Mom

P.S. I left the front door open. I guess you figured that out.

Dunkum put the note back on the counter. He stared out the kitchen window. "The thief might still be out there," he whispered.

He almost wished that rotten thief was lurking nearby. Dunkum would sneak up behind him. And grab his basketball right back!

FIVE

Dunkum leaned closer to the window. He watched for the slightest movement in his backyard. But no one was hiding in the bushes.

Then Dunkum had an idea. He would call Dee Dee Winters. She might know something. After all, she had the best view of his house. And . . . she had stayed home from church.

Dee Dee answered the phone. "Hello?"

"Have you seen anybody hanging around my house today?" Dunkum asked.

"Nope."

"Are you sure?" he asked.

"I'm sure," Dee Dee said.

"Well, you better lock your doors."

"How come?"

"Because there's a thief in the cul-de-sac."

Dee Dee gasped. "A thief! That's horrible!"

"Yes, and he robbed my house while we were at church," he said. "I better warn the rest of the kids." Dunkum said goodbye and hung up the phone.

Next, he called Jason, who lived next door to Dee Dee.

Br-r-ring!

"Hello?" Jason answered.

"Hey, Jason, you'd better keep your doors locked. There's a thief in the cul-de-sac."

"A what?" Jason yelled into the phone.

"A thief," Dunkum said. "And he just left my house!"

"How do you know?" Jason asked.

"He stole my new basketball," Dunkum said. "The one my uncle got for me from David Robinson."

Jason started laughing.

"Hey! It's not funny," Dunkum said.

"I know, I know," Jason said. "It's just so weird."

"How could the thief know where I hid it?" Dunkum said.

"It's real creepy," Jason whispered. Then he paused. "Hey, wait! I'm looking out my window. There's something blue stuck on your basketball pole."

Dunkum dropped the phone and ran outside. Jason was right! Dunkum peeled the blue paper off the pole. A bunch of dots and lines scampered across the page.

It looked like a secret code.

Who put it here? Dunkum wondered.

Then he saw a strange name at the bottom. Someone had signed it: CASE D. LUC.

"That's weird," Dunkum said out loud. "I don't know anyone by that name." He stared at the blue paper. There was some writing at the top. It said: IF YOU WANT YOUR BASKETBALL BACK, CRACK THIS CODE.

Dunkum stomped his foot. "Nothin's gonna stop me from getting my basketball back!" he shouted.

SIX

Dunkum saw Jason coming across the street. "Look at this!" Dunkum shouted. He waved the blue paper at his friend.

Jason pushed up his glasses and looked at the code. "I think it's the Morse Code."

Dunkum scratched his head. He studied the name at the bottom. "Who in the world is Case D. Luc?"

"This is crazy," Jason said.

"Can you help me crack the code?" Dunkum asked.

Jason shook his head. He had to go home for dinner. "Look in your encyclopedia," he called over his shoulder.

Rushing inside, Dunkum grabbed the encyclopedia. He found the page with the Morse alphabet:

A ● ▬
B ▬ ● ● ●
C ▬ ● ▬ ●
D ▬ ● ●
E ●
F ● ● ▬ ●
G ▬ ▬ ●
H ● ● ● ●
I ● ●
J ● ▬ ▬ ▬
K ▬ ● ▬
L ● ▬ ● ●
M ▬ ▬
N ▬ ●
O ▬ ▬ ▬
P ● ▬ ▬ ●

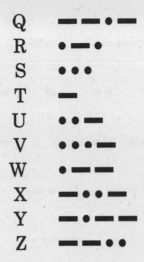

Q	— — • —
R	• — •
S	• • •
T	—
U	• • —
V	• • • —
W	• — —
X	— • • —
Y	— • — —
Z	— — • •

Dunkum studied the dots and dashes on the blue paper. (Can you crack the code before Dunkum does?)

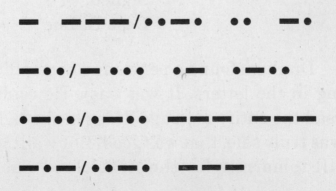

Signed,
Case D. Luc

Dunkum found a pencil and began fill-
ing in the letters. It was easy. He could
read the entire message. If his basketball
was truly safe, that was good. But waiting
till tomorrow for the next clue? That

38

wasn't good. Where would he find a gate—with a chalk mark?

Boom-a-bang! Thunder shook the house.

"Oh no!" cried Dunkum. "Not rain!" The chalk mark on the gate—wherever it was—might wash off.

What then?

SEVEN

The next day was Monday.

Dunkum woke up and reached for his basketball. He had forgotten it was gone. Sadly, Dunkum rubbed the sleep from his eyes. He ran to the window and looked out.

It was still raining!

Dunkum trudged downstairs. How would he find a chalk mark in the rain? His next clue depended on it!

★ ★ ★

After school, the rain had stopped.

Dunkum wasn't going to walk home with the Cul-de-sac Kids. Not today. He had an important mission to accomplish. A secret mission!

At home, Dunkum grabbed his after-school snack. Then he dashed outside to search for a gate. But where?

Dunkum knew of only one gate in the whole cul-de-sac. It was in Mr. Tressler's backyard. He was the old man who lived at the end of Blossom Hill Lane. The Cul-de-sac Kids had welcomed Mr. Tressler to the neighborhood last Christmas. Now he wasn't lonely anymore.

Dunkum headed for Mr. Tressler's house. He ran past Dee Dee's house. And Jason's. And Eric's.

At last he came to the end of the cul-de-sac. Marching up the steps, Dunkum headed for Mr. Tressler's doorbell. He rang it twice.

"Hello there, young man," the old gentleman said.

"Good afternoon," Dunkum said politely. "May I please look for something in your backyard?"

The man's face wrinkled into a smile. "Be my guest."

Dunkum thanked him and sprinted to the backyard. He headed for Mr. Tressler's back gate and searched for a chalk mark. There was no X mark near the latch. There was no X mark on either side of the gate.

Dunkum knelt in the damp grass. Then he spotted something. It was a chalky white X. "Yes!" he shouted.

Now where was the clue? Dunkum spotted an old flowerpot. Something was sticking out of the dirt. He pulled at it. But it was only a curled-up leaf.

But wait! Dunkum could see something yellow peeking out of the leaf. He opened it and found another code hidden inside.

Staring at the yellow paper, Dunkum

gulped. "There's no way I'll figure out *this* code," he said out loud.

"What's that you say?"

Dunkum stood up.

Mr. Tressler was calling to him from his deck. "What did you find out there?"

Dunkum ran across the yard with the yellow paper. Mr. Tressler looked puzzled when he saw the code. It was a bunch of strange shapes and symbols.

Then Dunkum told him about the missing basketball. And the first secret code—the Morse Code.

"A boy could get mighty lonely without his basketball," Mr. Tressler said. There was a twinkle in his eye.

"That ball means everything to me," Dunkum said.

"Everything? Even more than your friends in the cul-de-sac?" A wide grin swept across Mr. Tressler's face. "Seems to me, a ball is a poor exchange for friend-ship."

44

"I want to be a great player someday," Dunkum said. "Just like David Robinson. So, I have to keep practicing."

"What's wrong with your old ball?"

"It's not the same," said Dunkum. "David Robinson signed my new one!"

"I see," Mr. Tressler said, raising his eyebrows. "How can that make *you* play better?"

"It's fun to pretend. That's all," Dunkum said.

"Your friends are real, nothing pretend about them . . ." The old man's voice trailed off.

Dunkum blurted out, "My new basketball is more fun!"

Mr. Tressler lowered himself into a patio chair. He faced Dunkum squarely. "Well, now, how could a ball be more fun than Eric and Shawn and Abby and. . . ?"

Dunkum stood up. "I have important work to do," he said in a huff. "Excuse

45

me." And he ran out of the yard.

When he stopped to lock the gate, Dunkum saw something strange. Mr. Tressler was grinning!

EIGHT

Dunkum ran next door. "Is Eric home?" Dunkum asked Mrs. Hagel.

"He's riding bikes with Jason and Shawn," she said.

Dunkum sat down on Eric's step, thinking about Mr. Tressler. *Why was he grinning like that?*

Feeling quite lonely, Dunkum trudged across the street. Maybe Abby was home. He felt a lump in his throat as he knocked on her front door. He wished he hadn't yelled at her yesterday.

The door opened. It was Abby's little sister, Carly. "Hi, Dunkum." She had a stack of construction paper in her hands.

"Is Abby home?" Dunkum asked.

"She's at Stacy's house," Carly said.

Just then, Dee Dee came down the hall to sneak up on Carly. "Gotcha!" she shouted.

Carly jumped and the stack of colored papers fell to the floor.

Dunkum helped pick them up. When he started to hand a yellow page to her, he stopped. He looked at it. "Hey, wait a minute," Dunkum whispered to himself. "This paper looks the same as the one in my pocket!"

"Talking to yourself?" Dee Dee teased.

Dunkum held up the yellow construction paper. "Where did you get this?"

"The art supply store. Why?" Dee Dee asked.

Dunkum shook his head. "Just wondered."

"Carly and I are doing a project for school," Dee Dee said. "And we're going to get an A+! Right, Carly?"

Dunkum scratched his head and turned to go.

Carly closed the door. Dunkum pulled the yellow coded message out of his pocket. He stared at it. *Did Case D. Luc buy his paper at the same store as Dee Dee?* thought Dunkum.

Just then, Jimmy Hunter, Abby's little brother, came up the walk.

"Hi, Jimmy," Dunkum said. "Can you help me?" He felt silly asking a first grader for help. But he had no other choice. Everyone else was busy.

Jimmy pointed to himself. "Me?"

"Yes, you." Dunkum held up the yellow paper. He showed Jimmy the shapes on the latest code. "Have you ever seen anything like this?"

Jimmy nodded his dark head.

"You have? Where?" Dunkum shouted.

"Maybe you can help me crack this code."

"I not know about codes, but I see shapes in book," Jimmy said. "Wait!" He ran into the house. Soon he came back with a book. "Here." He shoved the book into Dunkum's hands.

Dunkum opened the library book. There were lots of codes inside. "Hey, thanks!" Dunkum patted Jimmy on the back.

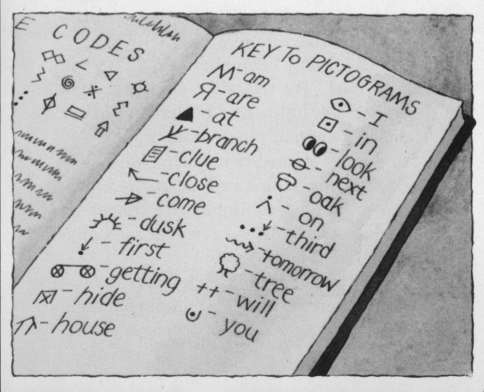

Jimmy grinned. "Open to first page."

Page one was a pictogram. Just like the code he'd found in Mr. Tressler's backyard!

NINE

Dunkum looked at the pictogram, then at Jimmy. "Where did you get this?"

"From sister's room."

"Which sister?" Dunkum said.

"Big sister. Abby sister."

"What's she doing with a code book?" Dunkum said, half to himself, and half to Jimmy.

Jimmy grinned. "Abby have pen pal. She write secret codes to Abby."

"Codes in a letter?" Dunkum said.

Jimmy nodded again. "Abby need book

to help her read secret messages."

Dunkum stuffed the yellow code into his shirt pocket. He wondered if Case D. Luc knew about this book.

Dunkum thanked Jimmy and hurried home. He didn't want to forget the pictograms in Abby's code book. Running into the house, he pulled the yellow paper out of his pocket. Dunkum began to fill in the blanks. (Can you finish before he does?)

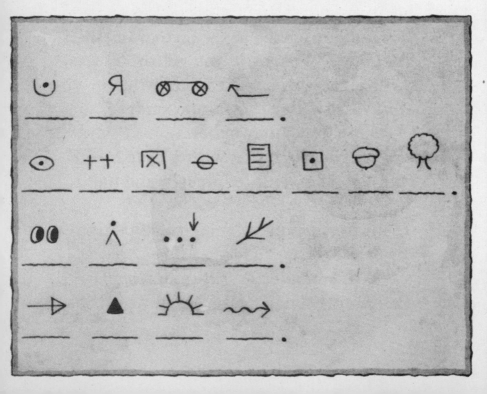

When he finished, the message was clear. Dunkum had to climb the old oak tree at the end of the cul-de-sac. Tomorrow the next clue would be waiting—on the third branch!

But waiting was hard for Dunkum. Twenty-four hours! How could he last another day without his basketball?

He watched for Eric, Jason, and Shawn from his front window. They would be back from riding bikes soon. Maybe he would ask them to come over and play. It had been a long time since he'd seen them.

After ten minutes, Dunkum gave up. He took some paper from the kitchen. Then he sat at the table and made a list of clues. He wrote a heading on his list.

THE MYSTERY OF CASE D. LUC

1. Basketball—signed by David Robinson
2. Basketball—stolen by Case D. Luc (???)

3. Blue Morse Code—found on backboard
4. Chalk mark on Mr. Tressler's gate
5. Yellow pictogram clue—found in flowerpot
6. Construction paper from art store—same as code paper
7. Library book—pictogram on first page
8. Next clue—tomorrow (in the old oak tree)

Dunkum twirled his pencil. He was determined to find this Case D. Luc person. He would never give up!

TEN

It was Tuesday—almost dusk.

Dunkum stared up at the old oak tree. He switched on his flashlight and pointed it up. He was dying to see his basketball sitting in the branches. But no basketball was in sight.

Up, up he climbed. Squatting down on the third branch, he looked around. No clues anywhere! He counted the branches again. 1 . . . 2 . . . 3! Nothing there.

Just then, Stacy Henry came by walking her dog, Sunday Funnies. She stopped under the lamppost. "What are you do-ing?" she called.

"Nothin' much," he answered.

Stacy walked toward him.

He wished she'd go away. He had to hunt for his next clue. In private!

"Want some company?" she asked. Be-fore he could say no, Stacy tied her dog to the tree. And she scrambled up to the third big branch.

Part of Dunkum wanted to tell her to leave. The other part wanted someone to talk to.

Soon Mr. Tressler's porch light came on. His house was closest to the oak tree.

"I wonder if Mr. Tressler's expecting someone," Stacy said.

"Maybe," Dunkum said, glancing over at the old man's house. "He gets lonely, I think."

"Yeah," Stacy said. "I'm glad he has the Cul-de-sac Kids to keep him com-pany."

"I wish *I* still did," Dunkum whispered.

Stacy smiled at him. Mr. Tressler's porch light helped Dunkum see her face. "You still have us," Stacy replied.

"It doesn't seem like it," Dunkum said sadly.

"Maybe you should come to the April Fool's Day party on Friday," she suggested. "It's going to be lots of fun."

Dunkum sighed. "Maybe I will."

Sunday Funnies began to whine.

Dunkum looked down at him from high in the tree. "Hey, look! Your dog's trying to get loose," he said.

Stacy laughed. "He likes to be where the action is. And right now, that's up here."

"Why don't you go down and bring him up?" Dunkum said. "Then he won't be lonely."

"I better not. It's getting dark," she said. "My mom might worry."

Dunkum was sorry to see Stacy leave. He watched her swing from one branch to another. Soon she was at the bottom, looking up.

"See you at school tomorrow." She waved goodbye.

Alone again, Dunkum leaned back against the tree trunk. He looked up at the stars. He thought about the April Fool's Day party. He thought about his cul-de-sac friends. A sad, sad feeling filled his heart.

Then Dunkum remembered why he was sitting in the tree. He looked again for the clue. In the dim light he saw a pink note, squished between two branches. *Why couldn't I find this before?* Dunkum wondered.

He opened the note and found a list of words. It looked like a grocery list. *Stacy must have dropped this,* Dunkum thought.

But where was the code?

ELEVEN

Dunkum scrambled down, out of the tree. He ran all the way to Stacy's house. Her mother might need the grocery list. He knocked on the door.

Stacy answered. "Hi, again."

"Did you drop your mom's grocery list?"

"What list? Where?" Stacy asked.

"In the tree." Dunkum showed her the paper.

"That's not my mom's list. Look, it has other words mixed in with the food

63

words," Stacy said. She stared at the paper.

Dunkum looked at the list, too.

crackers	oranges	peaches
yogurt	chips	potatoes
look	salsa	after
out	your	today
tower	man	spaghetti
apples	lettuce	school
on	baked beans	soup
shirt	bike	tomorrow

"That's strange. Could this be some kind of code?"

"Maybe," Stacy said. "I saw a code like this once. My uncle made it up. He called it a jumble code."

"What's that?" Dunkum asked.

"It's easy," Stacy said. "Each word in the secret message comes right *below* the food words. The rest of the words don't count."

"Oh, I get it."

Stacy ran into the house. She came back with a pencil. "Here, let's solve it together."

Dunkum paused. "Um, not now. But thanks."

"Why can't we work on it now?" she asked.

Dunkum scratched his head. "Sorry, Stacy. I better go home."

"Aw, please?" Stacy begged.

"I'll see you at school," Dunkum said. "Bye." He felt bad about leaving his friend like that. Stacy wasn't trying to snoop. He knew she just wanted to be a good friend.

Dunkum ran home to crack the code. When he finished it, the message was clear.

"Hey, wait a minute! How does Case D. Luc know I have a bike?"

"What did you say?" his mother said, coming down the steps.

"Nothin'," Dunkum muttered.

"Your friend Eric called," she said.

"He did?"

"He wants to play tomorrow."

"All right!" Dunkum shouted. "When?"

"After school." His mother grinned.

Dunkum spun around and aimed at the fireplace. He leaped up like he was shooting a basketball. He couldn't wait to see Eric again!

★ ★ ★

After school the next day, Dunkum greeted Eric. The boys rushed into the kitchen for some lemonade.

"Coming to Abby's party?" Eric asked.

"You bet!" Dunkum said.

"Changed your mind?" Eric asked.

Dunkum nodded. He didn't care about finding the next clue. It didn't matter now. Being with friends was much better.

At bedtime, Dunkum remembered the clue. Dashing downstairs, he looked in the garage. A green paper, folded like a

note, was taped to his bike. Dunkum
pulled the note off the seat. Strange-look-
ing words were written inside.

> EMOC OT ELOPGALF NI TNORF
> FO LOOHCS TA EERHT NO YA-
> DIRF. I LLIW GNIRB LLABTEK-
> SAB.
>
> > Signed,
> > Case D. Luc

How did this get here? Dunkum wondered. He studied the code for a long time.
Then he ran inside and held the green paper up to a mirror. The words were still
mixed up.

Finally, he figured it out. The words
weren't mirror image, they were back-
wards!

The message was: COME TO FLAG-
POLE IN FRONT OF SCHOOL AT
THREE ON FRIDAY. I WILL BRING
BASKETBALL.

Dunkum folded up the note. The April

67

Fool's Day party was at three o'clock, too. How could he meet Case D. Luc *and* go to the party?

Dunkum stared at the note. *What should I do?* he thought.

TWELVE

It was almost three o'clock on Friday. Time to meet Case D. Luc at the flagpole. And . . . time for the party at the end of the cul-de-sac.

Dunkum sat on his front porch. He thought about Case D. Luc and the codes. He thought about the Cul-de-sac Kids and the party. He missed his friends more than his new basketball. *Rats!* he thought. *Let Case D. Luc keep the silly ball.*

He ran to the end of the cul-de-sac.

Abby smiled. "Hi, Dunkum," she said. "Didn't you hear? We canceled the party."

Dunkum stepped back. "You what?"

Abby sat on the curb. "I'm sorry, Dunkum."

"But I just talked to Eric about it yesterday." Dunkum's heart was pounding. "And what about Stacy? She told me she was coming!"

"That's funny," Abby said, looking strange.

"It's *not* funny," Dunkum insisted.

Then—*Tap! Tap!* A familiar sound greeted Dunkum's ears. The Cul-de-sac Kids were coming out of their houses. They were all bouncing basketballs!

Dunkum turned to Abby. "What are they doing?"

"April Fool's, Dunkum!" she said. "The party is just beginning!"

The kids ran toward the oak tree, bouncing the balls. Dunkum was glad. He'd missed his friends. A lot!

Abby grabbed Dunkum's arm. "Look! There's Case D. Luc!"

Dunkum didn't see anyone new. "Where?"

Abby giggled. " 'Case D. Luc' is 'cul-de-sac' spelled backward."

Dunkum was puzzled. "Case D. Luc isn't some guy?"

"Nope," Abby said, grinning. "The Cul-de-sac Kids pulled a trick on you."

Dunkum couldn't believe it!

"We missed you, Dunkum. You were always playing basketball," she said. "We had to get your attention somehow."

"What a good trick," Dunkum said as he ran to meet the kids.

The Cul-de-sac Kids grabbed him. "April Fool's!" they shouted.

Dee Dee pushed her way through. "Here, Dunkum." She gave him the David Robinson basketball. "I was your thief."

Dunkum scratched his head. "*You* stole it?"

Dee Dee nodded.

"But how did you find it?" Dunkum asked.

"Easy," she said. "Your mom found it in your closet. I got it from her while you were at church."

"My parents helped you?" Dunkum said.

"We *all* helped," Eric spoke up. "I wrote the Morse Code on Dee Dee's blue construction paper."

"Mr. Tressler hid the yellow pictogram in his flowerpot," Abby said.

"And I marked the X on his gate," Jason said. "After it stopped raining." He jumped up and down holding the chalk.

Abby laughed. "I found the pictogram code in my library book."

At last, everything made sense.

Shawn smiled. "Stacy and I write jumble code."

Dunkum twirled the basketball on his pointer finger. He laughed with his friends. "I learned a good lesson. Thanks to Case D. Luc!"

The Cul-de-sac Kids cheered.

Stacy disappeared behind a bush. She came back carrying a tray. "Anybody hungry?"

"Everyone gets a menu first." Abby gave an orange-colored menu to each kid.

Jason passed around a box of pencils.

APRIL FOOL'S DAY MENU
(Draw a line to match the funny food with the answer.)

Ants on a Log
Silly Dillies
Jitter Blocks
Garden Pops
Sweet Hearts

strawberry Jell-O
gelatin cubes
heart-shaped mints
carrots
dill pickles
celery with peanut butter, topped with raisins

"Hey, this is fun!" Dunkum said. He

74

drew a line from Garden Pops to carrots. Then he chomped on one.

Abby pretended her raisins were ants—falling off the celery log and into her mouth.

Dee Dee squealed, "Oh, yuk!"

After the snacks were eaten, Abby made a suggestion. "Let's play basketball at the school."

Everyone agreed. The kids bounced their basketballs down the middle of the street. Dunkum led the way.

At the end of the cul-de-sac, Dunkum glanced over his shoulder. There was a message written on Abby's T-shirt. It said: CUL-DE-SAC KIDS STICK TO-GETHER!

Dunkum dribbled his ball hard and fast. *Case D. Luc, you're terrific!* he thought.

Then the Cul-de-sac Kids crossed the street to Blossom Hill School.

Together!

ABOUT THE AUTHOR

Beverly Lewis wrote lots of secret codes in Pennsylvania, where she grew up. She liked to hide them, too—sometimes in very strange places. Now Beverly writes notes to her husband and kids in pictograms. The notes are often found in drawers, on the piano, or stuck to a mirror.

Beverly enjoys getting letters from her readers. Watch out, she might send you a letter in code!

Look for other chapter books by Beverly Lewis: *The Six-Hour Mystery* and *Mystery at Midnight*.

THE CUL-DE-SAC KIDS SERIES
Don't miss #7!

THE STINKY SNEAKERS MYSTERY

Jason's back—and bragging about his cool science fair project. Can alfalfa sprouts *really* grow in a carpet square?

On the day of the fair, Jason's "super sprouts" disappear. Will Miss Hershey give him a big, fat zero? Jason scrambles to do a last-minute project with wacky results.

Then, during P.E., globs of rotten-smelling cheese show up in the Cul-de-sac Kids' sneakers. Who would do such a thing? And why?

Also by Beverly Lewis

Adult Nonfiction
Amish Prayers
The Beverly Lewis Amish Heritage Cookbook

Adult Fiction
HOME TO HICKORY HOLLOW
The Fiddler • *The Bridesmaid* • *The Guardian*

SEASONS OF GRACE
The Secret • *The Missing* • *The Telling*

ABRAM'S DAUGHTERS
The Covenant • *The Betrayal* • *The Sacrifice* • *The Prodigal* •
The Revelation

ANNIE'S PEOPLE
The Preacher's Daughter • *The Englisher* • *The Brethren*

THE ROSE TRILOGY
The Thorn • *The Judgment* • *The Mercy*

THE COURTSHIP OF NELLIE FISHER
The Parting • *The Forbidden* • *The Longing*

THE HERITAGE OF LANCASTER COUNTY
The Shunning • *The Confession* • *The Reckoning*

OTHER ADULT FICTION
The Postcard • *The Crossroad* • *The Redemption of Sarah
Cain* • *October Song* • *Sanctuary** • *The Sunroom*

Youth Fiction
Girls Only (GO!) Volume One and *Volume Two*†
SummerHill Secrets Volume One and *Volume Two*†
Holly's Heart Collection One‡, *Collection Two*‡,
and *Collection Three*†

www.BeverlyLewis.com

*with David Lewis   †4 books in each volume   ‡5 books in each volume

From Bethany House Publishers

Fiction for Young Readers

(ages 7–10)

ASTROKIDS™
by Robert Elmer

Space scooters? Floating robots? Jupiter ice cream? Blast into the future for out-of-this-world, zero-gravity fun with the AstroKids on space station *CLEO-7*.

THE CUL-DE-SAC KIDS
by Beverly Lewis

Each story in this lighthearted series features the hilarious antics and predicaments of nine endearing boys and girls who live on Blossom Hill Lane.

JANETTE OKE'S ANIMAL FRIENDS
by Janette Oke

Endearing creatures from the farm, forest, and zoo discover their place in God's world through various struggles, mishaps, and adventures.